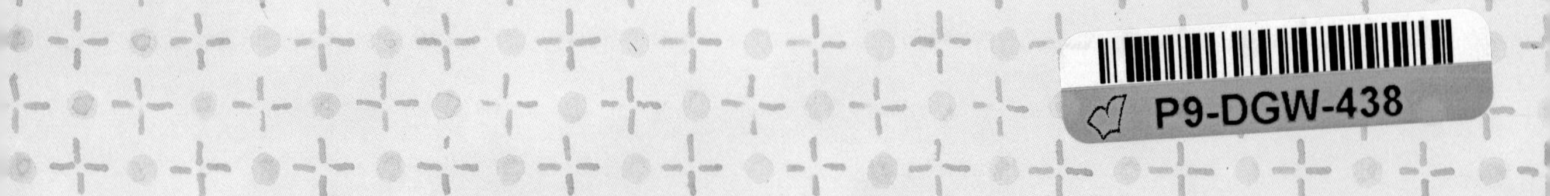
P9-DGW-438

Ann Jonas
Where Can It Be?

Greenwillow Books/New York

To Amy, who inspired this book,
and to Nina, who helped create it.

Printed in Japan by
Dai Nippon Printing Co.
First Edition
10 9 8 7 6 5 4 3 2 1

Library of Congress
Cataloging-in-Publication Data
Jonas, Ann. Where can it be?
Summary: A child looks all over the house for her missing blanket.
[1. Lost and found possessions
—Fiction] I. Title.
PZ7.J664Wi 1986 [E] 86-304
ISBN 0-688-05169-3
ISBN 0-688-05246-0 (lib. bdg.)

Watercolor paints and colored pencils were used for the full-color art.
The typeface is Helvetica Bold.

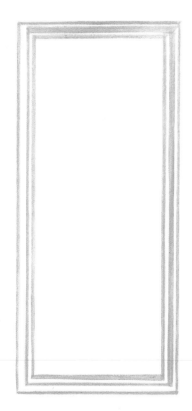

I don't know
where I left it.
I'm sure I brought it
home with me.
I have to find it!

I'll look in my closet!

Just my clothes.

I'll look in my cupboard!

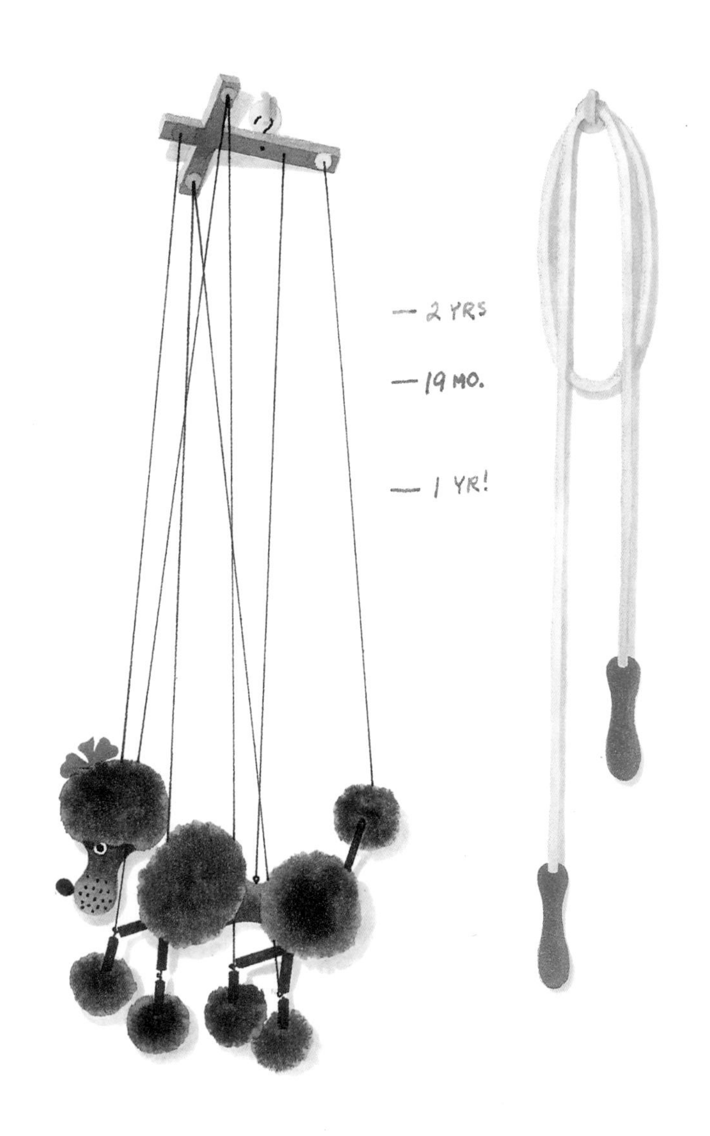
— 2 YRS
— 19 MO.
— 1 YR!

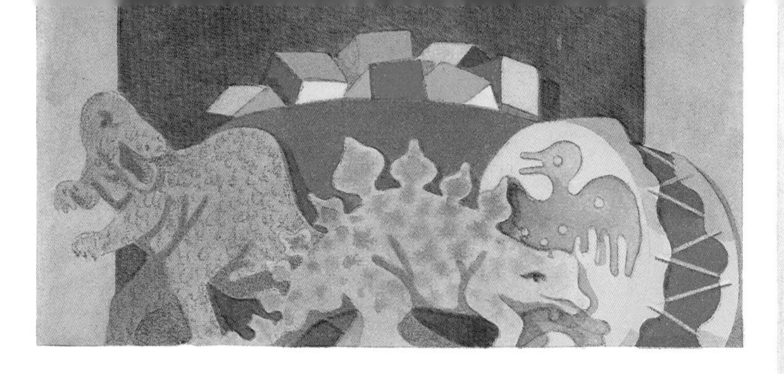

Just my toys.

I'll look in my bed!

Just my cat.

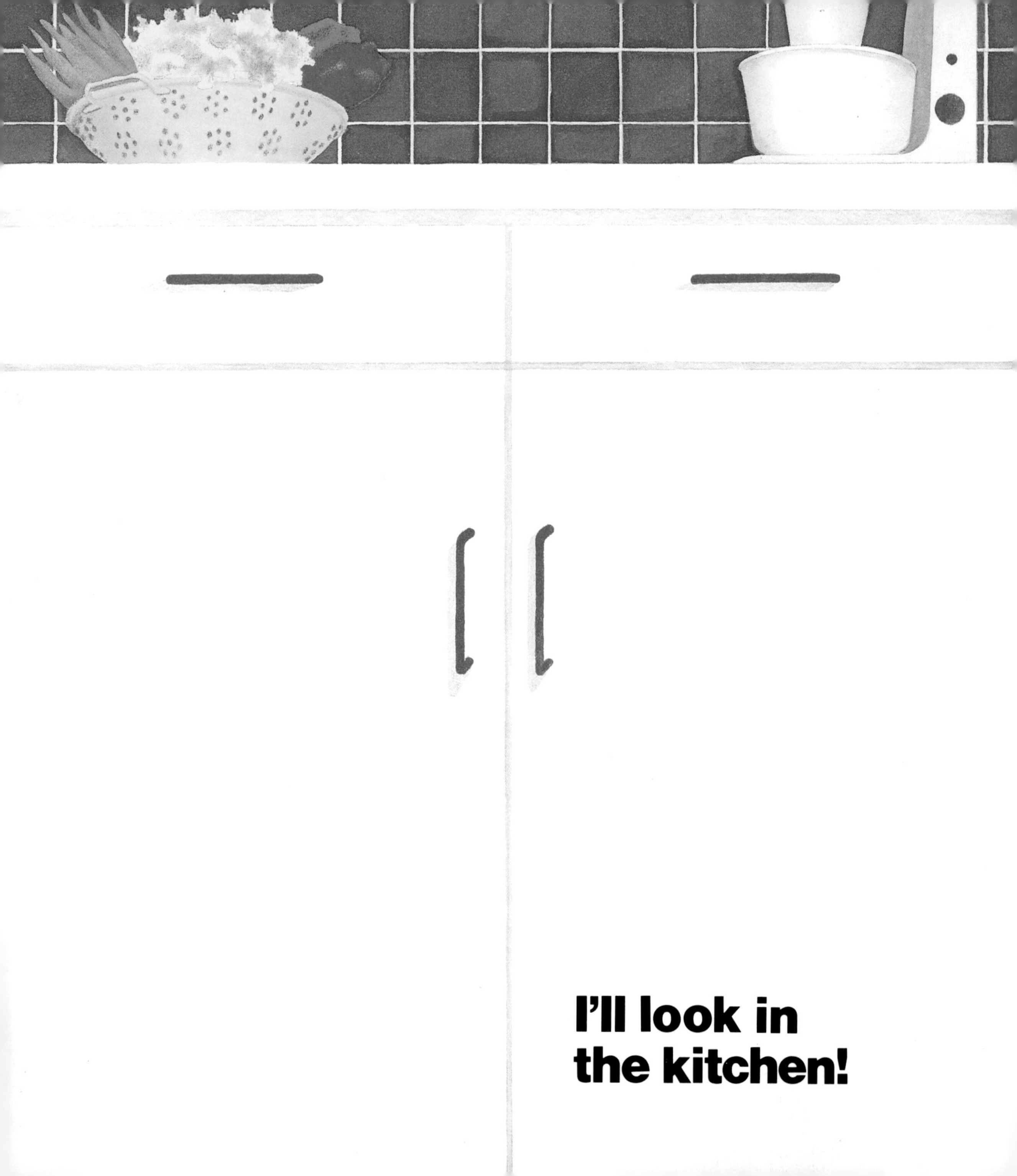

I'll look in the kitchen!

Just pots.

I'll look in the refrigerator!

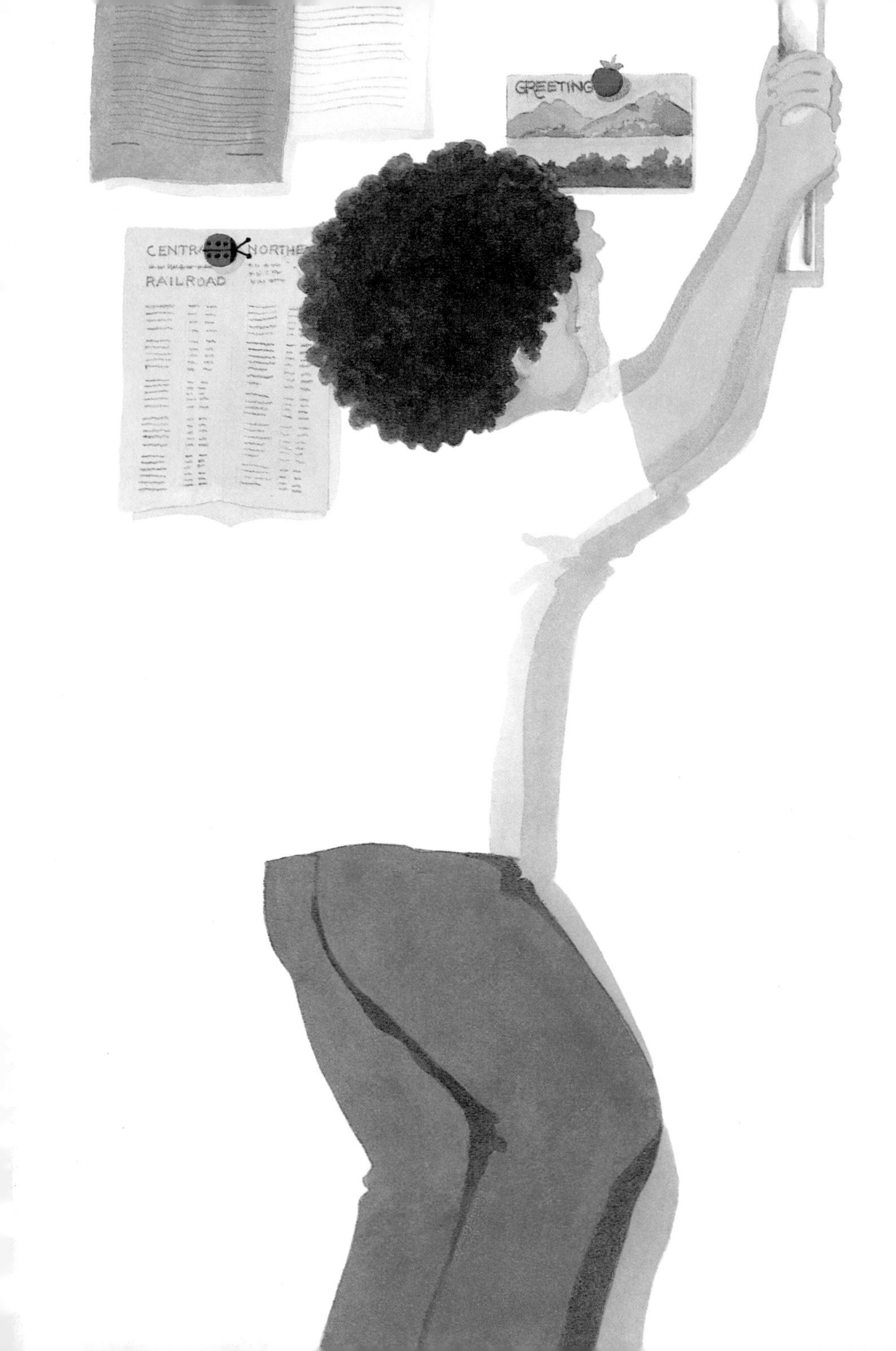
GREETING
RAILROAD

BUTTER
CHEESE
JELLY
FIZZO
TOMATO
JUICE

Just cold food.

I'll look under the table!

Just my cat again.

Maybe I left it at Deborah's house. The doorbell is ringing.

780
LETTERS

It's Deborah and

my blanket!